The Mean Girl Who

DETECTIVE DOVE

ZUNI BLUE

AMARIA & SARIEL

LONDON

THE MEAN GIRL WHO NEVER SPEAKS

Cover Illustration by Fenny Fu

For more information, please contact:

Zuni Blue at www.zuniblue.com

Print ISBN: 978-1097689934

First Edition August 2013

This Edition May 2019

100 Free Gifts For You

There are 100 FREE printables waiting for you!

Certificates, bookmarks, wallpapers and more! You can choose your favourite colour: red, yellow, pink, green, orange, purple or blue.

You don't need money or an email address. Check out www.zuniblue.com to print your free gifts today.

CONTENTS

Case File No.1

In London, England, you'll find Detective Inspector Mya Dove. With four years' experience on the police force, this eight-year-old is on her way to being the best police officer ever.

Yes. The best. Her mum said so.

To inspire other kids, she's sharing case files. Case File No.1: The Mean Girl Who Never Speaks.

Chapter 1

The week started with a tough Maths lesson. I thought Maths was bad last year, but it was worse now. I missed just adding up and taking away small numbers. Now we had to multiply and divide by twelve too!

"No calculator allowed," our teacher Mrs Cherry said. "You've got to use your heads!"

How could we concentrate when it was so early in the morning? Some sunshine would've made us feel better, but it was cold, dark and rainy outside.

"Just do your very best, children," Mrs Cherry said happily. "Isn't Maths fun?"

"Yes, Mrs Cherry," we all said.

Mrs Cherry smiled. She really enjoyed giving us hard work. At least she was having a good time, I guess. Nobody else was.

"Detective Inspector?" Someone whispered behind me. "I've got a note for you!"

When Mrs Cherry wasn't looking, I quickly turned back and grabbed the note from my classmate's hand. I slipped it into my skinny, black pencil case. It was my favourite pencil case because when people saw it, they took me very seriously. They used to laugh at my old pencil case. It was sparkly, bright pink and had cute bunny rabbits on it.

"Is there a problem, Mya?" Mrs Cherry asked, her narrow, brown eyes on me. "This is not a group exercise. No talking, please."

"We weren't talking, Miss," I said. "I sneezed. He gave me a tissue."

"That's odd," Mrs Cherry said. "I didn't hear you sneeze..." She raised her bushy, red eyebrows. Whenever she did that, she had lots of wrinkles on her forehead. I heard she was thirty, but the wrinkles made her look really, really old, like forty or something. "Anyway, children, back to work."

Maths was very important, but I had other work to do. The note would tell me what I needed to know, but I couldn't read it in class. Mrs Cherry was nosy like lots of grown-ups, so she'd want to see what I was reading. Then everyone would know what I was up to...

I needed to read the note somewhere private and quiet, so I could concentrate.

"Can I go to the toilet, please?" I asked, giving my sad face. "I've really gotta go!"

Mrs Cherry nodded and her bushy eyebrows went down. The wrinkles disappeared.

I put the note in my pocket and walked to the toilet. Walking is so slow but running got me into trouble last time.

"Health and Safety," Mr Badal had snapped. "You could trip over and fall and hurt yourself. Then your parents will blame the school!"

I had to listen to him. He was the meanest Headteacher in the whole world, probably even the whole universe. He was rude to the teachers, students, cleaners, dinner ladies...everyone except our parents.

It took forever walking so slowly to the bathroom, but finally I made it. Usually the toilets were very stinky. Unfortunately, today someone had done a poo! Fortunately, my secret police boss had sprayed some perfume before I got there. Now I could smell poo and flowers.

Flowery poo.

The first toilet door was locked. Someone was in there. I went into the next toilet down and locked the door. I waited a minute or two, just in case someone might be listening. I didn't hear any voices, so I knew it was safe to talk.

I stomped my foot three times.

The person in the next toilet stomped twice.

Then I stomped once.

"What's the password?" the girl next door whispered.

"Children's Police Force," I said.

"Good...Now read the note."

I took it out. Here's what it said:

To Detective Inspector Mya Dove,

The Children's Police Force needs your help. It's time for your first big case.

There's a new girl at school. She'll be joining your class. Her name is Libby Smith.

On her first day, Libby looked okay. Her mum talked to other mums. Her dad talked to your dad. Her big sister talked to Mrs Cherry.

But...Libby's mean. She hasn't said ANYTHING yet, but she's obviously mean. That's why she still doesn't have any friends and she's been here for ages (two weeks!).

We wanna be fair, so we want you to make sure she's mean. If she is, we'll start telling other kids not to be her friend. If she isn't mean, we'll stop any rumours about her that we started.

Your reward will be a big bag of grapes.

If you have any questions, just ask.

Now stop reading and get to work!

Regards,

Your Secret Boss

P.S. I said STOP reading and GET TO WORK!!!!!!

Why were grapes my reward instead of money, chocolate or sweets? What kid doesn't want chocolate instead of fruit? Okay, okay, let me explain...

I like chocolate and sweets, but what I really LOVE are grapes. The green ones. I can't eat too many because they make me poo a lot. Not just any poo. They're sloppy ones that shoot out. Then I have to clean the toilet AND wash my hands. That's too much work.

"Grapes?" I asked. "Are they the green ones?"

"There are no green grapes. You mean white grapes."

"No," I snapped. "The green ones."

"Yeah, they're WHITE grapes," she snapped back. "They look green but they're white grapes."

"Look, boss, I am not Detective Inspector for no reason! Don't try and trick me!" I tried not to cry. "Just give me green grapes, okay? I know my colours. I wouldn't mix up green and white. They're totally different!"

"But—"

"You can't trick me, okay? I know green grapes when I see them. You know what? Maybe YOU are the meanie, not the new girl!"

She dropped a plastic bag and slid it

under the toilet stall.

Inside were ten juicy GREEN grapes. So round. So firm. So mine.

"They look so tasty," I said. "Add another grape and I'll solve the case."

"Done!"

She reached under the toilet stall and held out her hand. She wanted to shake hands so we had a deal.

"Wash your hands first," I said. "If I catch germs, I'll be sick. I can't work if I'm sick."

"If you get sick, you'll have a week off school. Think about it. Cartoons, brekkie in bed, and no homework."

She had a point...

"I can't," I said. "Just get my extra grape...and please find out who keeps doing a poo in here! It's smells so bad."

"It's definitely not me..." She

sprayed more perfume. "Excuse me."

"So, um..."

"What, Inspector? Spit it out!"

"Are you gonna tell me who you are?"

"Definitely not."

I didn't bother arguing. I'd tried that already. This girl was my boss, but she wouldn't tell me who she was. We only met in the bathroom and she never showed her face. As long as she gave me cases to solve, I didn't mind not meeting her face-to-face.

"Could I meet the Children's Police Force, please?" I asked.

"You know better than to ask that!" she snapped.

But it was worth a try!

The Children's Police Force included millions of kids worldwide.

They had officers in Europe, North America, South America, Africa, Asia, Australia, the North Pole and the South Pole.

I was part of the Children's Police Force in London, England. They sent me a secret note in class, inviting me to join. They chose me because I'd been finding my own cases and solving every one!

If I helped the Children's Police Force, I might be invited to the real police someday! Then I could solve even bigger cases.

"Detective Inspector Mya Dove, are you daydreaming again?"

"Yes...I mean, no!"

"Good," she snapped. "Now get back to class!"

After saying goodbye to my grapes, I

returned to class. Mrs Cherry raised an eyebrow because I'd taken so long in the toilets, but she said nothing.

I finished my Maths work as fast as I could. If you finish early, you get to sit around and wait for everyone else. Instead of staring out the window like other kids, I took out my notepad and pencil and started writing.

Libby Smith, I wrote. New girl. Is she mean? Maybe...Maybe not.

This was going to be tough. I hadn't had a case in a long time (three whole weeks) so I needed some practice. I needed some help too.

And I knew just who to ask...

Chapter 2

One time my secret boss told me there were other Children's Police Force officers at school. I could always get help if I needed it. My boss couldn't just give out the officers' names. You never know who might be listening in the toilets!

"Could you give me a clue?" I asked. "Just tell me where to find one Children's Police Force officer, please. I might need some help with a case!"

"If you ever need help, check the

football pitch," she said. "There's a Children's Police Force officer there. You'll know him when you see him..."

That was easier said than done. In the playground, there were thirty boys playing football (some people call football "soccer"). I stayed off the pitch and looked for the secret police officer, but couldn't see him. It's hard to find someone when you don't know who you're looking for!

Was the secret police officer the black boy keeping score? That would be a great way to stay undercover. He could look out for any bad guys on both teams.

Or was the secret police officer the goalie? Football is boring when no one scores! But if no one scored, the goalie would have lots of time to pick out bad guys.

Or was the secret police officer the spotty-faced, white boy who kept slowing down when he passed me? He ran to the water fountain and drank for a VERY long time. He stared at me. And stared. And stared. Then he winked at me three times.

Nah, I thought. Not him.

"Over here!" he shouted, waving me over. "Yeah, you! Come here!"

"What do you want?" I asked, staying where I was.

"You needed help with something?"

He winked.

I walked over to him.

He said, "We're in the same class, cool! I'm Jimmy! What's your—"

"Great game!" I shouted. "Any good tips?"

"...What're you doing?"

"Act natural," I whispered. "Bad guys might be watching."

"You're right, sorry!"

"Any tips about the mean girl case?" I whispered.

"Not here," he whispered. "The bad guys might hear us. Follow me."

He pulled me behind the football net and held out his sweaty hand.

"Pay up," he said.

"But—"

"Pay up!"

Adult police officers don't pay each other for information, but at my school we did. It'd always been like that. I decided that when I got to Year Six, I'd change the rules. Then the Children's Police Force would help each other for free.

I gave Jimmy five pence.

"Ten," he said, "or I'm not telling you anything!"

When I was younger, police tips only cost two pence. The price had gone up a lot in four years.

I gave him another five pence and he held it close to his eye. Then he bit it hard and his baby tooth popped out.

"It's real money," he said, popping his tooth back in. "Can't be too sure these days. Last week a kid gave me chocolate money."

He put the money in his trainer.

"Who's your suspect?" he asked.

"Libby Smith."

"Libby Sam Smith or Libby Charlie Smith or—"

"I don't know! Why'd you think I paid you? I need info!"

"Okay, fine. I'll ask some questions. Then I can figure out which Libby you're talking about. Got it?"

I nodded.

"First off, what's your name?"

"Detective Inspector Mya Dove."

"I remember you from class," he said. "Anyway, when did Libby Smith get here?"

"Two weeks ago."

"So she's a new girl..." He pulled out a tiny notebook from his t-shirt pocket and looked down a list of names. "Is she on probation?"

"...What's does "probation" mean?"

"Never mind," he said. "Is she black, white or Asian or another race?"

"White like you, I think. Or black like me. Or Asian or biracial or...don't know."

"Okay...Is she tall or short?"

"Tall, maybe. Short, maybe. Maybe in the middle somewhere." I shrugged. "I don't know that one either. Sorry."

He closed the notebook, giving me an angry look. I was feeling a bit angry too. Why didn't my secret boss give me more info? How could I find Libby Smith when I didn't know what she looked like?

"Is Libby even a girl?" he asked. "Do you know that one?"

"No. I don't."

He walked off in a huff, so I ran after him and pulled him back.

"I was just joking," I said. "Of course Libby's a girl!"

"I take my job very seriously." He glared at me. "You should too."

Ouch! That hurt a little...

"Wait a minute," I said. "My boss said she's moving to our class?"

"Why didn't you say so before?" he cried. "I know which Libby Smith you're talking about. She's been studying in Mr Badal's office since her first day. Nobody knows why..."

He took my hand and led me down the playground. People were staring, but I didn't care. His hand felt so soft. I liked holding it.

"We're gonna walk past her," he said. "Act natural."

"Walk past who?"

"Libby Smith."

This was it. The moment I'd been waiting for. I was about to meet Libby Smith, the suspect in my case.

"This will be easy," I said. "I've met lots of mean girls before."

All I had to do was prove Libby was mean. I thought it would be easy, but I was very wrong.

"Libby isn't like other mean girls," Jimmy said. "She's *different*."

"What do you mean?" I asked.

"You'll see..."

Chapter 3

I was very excited. I was about to meet Libby Smith for the first time. Even better, I got to hold Jimmy's warm hand while we walked together, pretending to chat. Sometimes police officers have to pretend so bad guys don't know what we're up to.

There was a black girl straight ahead, her eyes on us. Then she looked away and stared at the ground when we went past.

Then Jimmy let go.

"You saw her?" he asked.

"Yeah..." My hand felt cold without his.

"If you need help again, let me know. I charge from ten pence up to a pound."

A whole pound? What a rip off!

"A pound? For what?"

"Anything that could get me into really, really serious trouble," he said. "Remember when Mr Badal got locked out of his office? Remember the toy mouse in Mrs Cherry's desk drawer? Remember when the exams almost got cancelled?"

"Wow...Thanks to you I had extra time to study!"

"Just give me a sign, okay? I'm always about."

He ran back to the football pitch.

I sat on the bench nearest to Libby and pretended to read my notepad. Actually I was keeping an eye on her.

Libby's hair was afro like mine but she'd straightened it. She didn't have any pretty hairbands like Angel, the meanest girl in school, but she did have a lovely yellow dress.

It was a very pretty dress, but why wear it to school? Maybe because Libby had lots of money? Angel was rich and mean, so maybe Libby was rich and mean too.

Libby didn't have anything to play with. No balls. No hula hoops. No skipping rope. All she did was stand in the middle of the playground. Whenever someone smiled at her, she looked away.

Why didn't she smile back?

All breaktime she stayed alone. If anyone got too close, she quickly moved away. I tried to catch her eye but she pretended not to see me, so I decided to go right up to her.

But the bell rang.

Time to go back inside.

Libby sighed with relief. She joined the line back to class, keeping her eyes to the ground.

Why was she staying by herself all the time? Maybe because she didn't like us?

It was easy to stay alone at breaktime, but soon she'd have no choice but to talk to someone. Our next lesson was P.E. (P.E. is Physical Education class, remember?). Teamwork was an important part of P.E. class.

"I'm gonna talk to her," I told myself.

Ten minutes later, we were in the hall. It was the same hall we used for lunch, so sometimes the floor was a bit messy. We didn't mind, though. P.E. was a great time to have some fun.

It was also a great time to solve top secret cases. Why? Because playtime and P.E. were the only times we could do whatever we liked!

Anyway, it was time to choose P.E. teams. Everyone wanted me on their team because I always keep fit. The police have to keep fit so we can chase bad guys.

"Mya, over here!"

"Join our team, Mya!"

"No! Come here!"

"DON'T come over here, Mya!"

That was Angel. She was mean to everyone but the teachers. She was always very nice to them. Probably because kids who are mean to teachers get detention.

Everyone looked very disappointed when I turned them down. I didn't want to, but I had to. Today I was only pairing up with one person: Libby Smith.

I found her at the back of the hall. She was shooting a basketball and making every shot. I was really impressed by her dribbling skills. If she'd talk to people, she could play on any team she liked.

But as soon as she noticed me watching, she started missing shots. One shot bounced off the rim. Another one smacked the backboard. Then the ball flew past the net.

Maybe she's pretending to be bad so I won't play with her, I thought. That's something a mean person would do, right?

When I got closer, she picked up a skipping rope and just stood with it. I rushed to the other end and picked it up. I tried turning it, but she wouldn't do it with me. She just stood there, her hands shaking like she felt chilly.

We stood in silence for a minute or two. I looked at her. She looked down at her shoes. I waited a few seconds, but she wouldn't look up. I had to say something before the lesson was over.

"Hello, Libby," I said. "I'm Mya. You're in our class now. Maybe we can be friends?"

I thought she'd say hello back.

Instead, something very strange happened...

Chapter 4

Libby Smith kept looking at her shoes.

"Um, HELLO," I said. "My name is Mya. What's yours?"

She mumbled something and turned away, dropping the rope.

How rude!

"We can play together if you just talk to me," I said. "Can't you say hello?"

She rushed away to Mrs Cherry. I followed her over but then Mrs Cherry took her into the corridor and closed the door behind them.

I pressed my ear against the door, but it was hard hearing Mrs Cherry and Libby talk over my noisy class. I stuck my finger in my other ear and managed to hear Libby crying.

"Are you seriously falling for that?" Angel asked, appearing from nowhere. I turned to face her.

"Am I falling for what?" I asked. "What are you talking about?"

"She's faking it," Angel snapped. "Crybabies cry when they don't get what they want."

"Maybe she's really upset?"

"She's a really mean girl," Angel said. "Trust me. I can feel it in my curls."

"You mean you can feel it in your BONES, not your curls."

"Whatever!"

If Angel said Libby was bad, Libby was REALLY bad. Until Libby came, Angel was the meanest person in the whole school. That's why I didn't want to be Angel's friend.

Police officers aren't friends with bad guys or girls like Angel. If the Children's Police Force thought I was friends with her, they'd never give me another case!

"Mya, are you listening to me?" Angel snapped, tapping her foot.

She wasn't just mean but annoying too. The boys at school didn't like her. The girls didn't like her either. All because she was so mean, but she thought we were just jealous.

"Everyone's jealous because I'm so pretty and have so much money," she'd say. "I am so lucky! And so pretty! I'm pretty lucky!"

Angel had big, curly blonde hair and bright pink cheeks. People said she looked so sweet, even though she wasn't sweet at all. Her mum got her the prettiest dresses because they had lots of money.

"You're not listening to me, are you?" Angel spat. "You're jealous too! You wish you looked like me."

No, I didn't.

Angel looked nothing like me.

I'm black with really long, coily afro hair. When my mum blow-dried my hair, it ended up fluffy like candy floss. I loved it! Unlike Angel's white skin, my dark brown skin never changed colour.

"Mya, I'm talking to you!" Angel

cried. "Answer me!"

Angel and I wore different clothes too. She wore fluffy pink dresses and shiny pink shoes and sparkly pink hairbands. I liked plain white shirts, dark trousers and black shoes. Being smartly dressed is what good police officers do.

"Are you listening to me?" Angel snapped. "MYA! HELLO!"

"I'm listening..."

"Anyway, I just said that Libby never says good morning or goodbye. She doesn't answer the register either. She doesn't answer questions in class."

Nobody HAD to answer questions in class, but usually Mrs Cherry would ask everyone at least one question.

"Teachers are supposed to introduce the new student to class," Angel said.

"Mrs Cherry didn't tell us about Libby. She just showed up and most of you didn't even notice! Probably because she doesn't speak..."

"Can she talk?" I asked. "Some people can't."

"She talks but I don't know what she's saying. She mumbles...You know what? I bet she's talking about me!" Angel flicked her curls. "All you jealous girls are talking about me!"

I rolled my eyes and walked away from her. I didn't speak to her unless I absolutely had to because she was SO annoying!

But she had been helpful. Based on what she'd told me, Libby stayed alone and didn't talk to anyone because she was mean. That meant my case had been solved. I'd proven Libby was mean, so I'd get rewarded with juicy GREEN grapes!

Jimmy came over with the basketball and we started playing. I was good at shooting, but he was even better.

"How'd it go?" he asked.

"I think Libby is crying."

"That sucks. Is she okay?"

"Of course. Mrs Cherry is with her." I tried to grab the basketball but Jimmy dribbled it away from me. "Libby doesn't talk or play with anyone else. That's a mean thing to do."

Jimmy took a shot and got three points. Out of breath, we both sat down on the bench for a break.

I kept an eye on the door, waiting for Libby to come back in.

A minute later, Mrs Cherry rushed back into the hall and blew her whistle.

We all gathered around her.

"Class, I have to pop out for a few minutes. I will be in Mr Badal's office." She looked each one of us in the eye. "Behave yourselves. I do not want any trouble, understood?"

"Yes, Miss," we all said.

Mrs Cherry hurried back out. The door slowly closed behind her. I could see Libby sitting on the floor with her head in her hands.

Suddenly I felt a bit...*guilty*.

"You see that?" Jimmy asked me. "Libby is still crying. It must be pretty bad."

"Mean girls fake cry," I said. "Angel does it too."

"They don't fake cry when no one's looking. They only do it for attention. You can't get attention when no one else is there."

He was right.

Jimmy started bouncing the basketball and took another shot. Another three points scored. I was way behind now.

I expected him to run over and grab the basketball, but he didn't. Instead he turned to me with a sad look on his face.

"Mya, are you sure she's mean?"

"Yep. My girl secret boss said so."

"My boy secret boss said so too, but what do YOU think?"

I hadn't really sat down and thought about it much. It was my job to help the Children's Police Force. That meant solving my case and getting my grapes. Simple as that.

"I dunno," I said. "I just want my

grapes."

"Mya, being a good police officer means being a good person. Don't forget that."

What was *that* supposed to mean?

Before I could ask, he ran off to play handball with some boys.

"Fine, then," I said to myself. "I'm going to ask Libby if she's mean. When she says yes, I'll tell my secret boss the case is closed. Soon I'll be eating those juicy grapes. I might share one or two..."

"Mya, come play with us!" a friend cried.

I glanced at the door. Mrs Cherry and Libby should've been back by now. I couldn't sit around waiting anymore. It was too boring.

"I'm coming," I said, running over

to play cricket. “I’m on the blue team!”

Libby didn’t come back to P.E. class, but I didn’t notice. I was too busy playing with my friends.

I wasn’t thinking about police work anymore. I thought the mean girl case was over, but I was wrong. Very wrong...

Chapter 5

At breaktime, I couldn't find Libby in the playground. I looked for her under the climbing frame., inside the toybox and even behind the tree. She wasn't playing ball games with the boys and Sam the tomboy. She wasn't with the girls playing hula hoop either.

"She's hiding," I told myself. "I'll catch her in class."

When we got back to class, she wasn't there either!

Her desk was empty, but her name

tag was still on it. That meant she was coming back. She hadn't left school for good, but where was she?

Libby disappearing wasn't the only surprise. Jimmy had moved desks. Now he was next to me at the back.

"Pst! Jimmy!" I whispered. "Nod if you can hear me!"

When Mrs Cherry wasn't looking, he quickly nodded.

"Have you seen Libby Smith?" I asked.

Mrs Cherry started writing on the whiteboard. She always wrote a lot, so we had time to talk.

"I saw her with Emma," he said. "In the playground."

"Were they talking?" I asked, shocked to hear that Libby might have a friend.

"Nah, Libby just followed Emma around the playground for a bit. Everywhere Emma went, Libby went. They didn't talk or anything."

"Then what happened?"

"Emma looked angry and told Libby to stop following her. Libby started crying. Emma said sorry, but Libby ran inside and wouldn't come back out."

Libby seemed to cry a lot. I couldn't remember other mean people crying a lot. Mean people shouted and hurt people, just like Angel always did.

"Why was she following Emma like that?"

"I don't know..."

Jimmy wouldn't look me in the eye. Usually when people do that, they're lying or hiding something.

"You can tell me," I whispered. "Go

on. I won't tell my secret boss, I promise."

"Well, I think Libby followed Emma around because she was...*lonely*. Libby finally had someone to hang out with."

"So Libby just wanted a friend?" I whispered. "You don't make friends following people around like that. It's weird!"

"I don't think Libby meant it in a weird way. Libby probably wanted some company, you know? It's hard being alone all the time."

Jimmy looked really sad when he talked about Libby. It was like he felt sorry for her, but why? People said she was mean. You shouldn't feel sorry for mean people. You should feel sorry for the people they're mean to.

"Do you really think she's mean?"

Jimmy asked. "Be honest. I won't tell anyone."

"I…Well…Um…"

I wasn't sure what to think, but what I thought didn't matter anyway. I was supposed to show Libby was mean. Once I did that, I'd get my juicy grapes to eat.

Mrs Cherry finally finished writing on the board and we got to work. Luckily it was a small group exercise. Jimmy and I decided to work together. It was a chance for us to chat some more.

"Mya, have you looked everywhere for Libby?" Jimmy asked. "*Everywhere?*"

"Yes."

"All over the playground?"

"Yes."

"The lunch hall?"

"Yes."

"The toilets?"

"...Not yet," I said. "I was going there next."

"What about the staff room?"

I hadn't thought of that one. Sometimes kids got to study in the staff room, but only when teachers were off sick.

When a teacher was sick, sometimes their class was split into smaller groups. Each group went to a different classroom. Anyone left over got to work in the staff room. Otherwise, students weren't allowed in there.

"Check the girls' toilets," Jimmy said. "I'll check the boys', all right?"

"Why would Libby be in the boys' toilets?"

Jimmy shrugged.

As soon as the lesson was over, Jimmy and I rushed to the toilets. He went into the boys' and came out a minute or so later. He shook his head.

Time to check the girls' toilets.

Libby Smith, I thought. I'm coming in and there's nowhere you can hide. I am going to prove you're mean and get my grapes.

I marched into the bathroom, expecting to see Libby Smith. Instead, there was someone else waiting for me...

Chapter 6

The toilets. Where else can you get some quiet time at school? No one bothers you in the loo. That's why I wrote my case files in there.

I even had my own DO NOT DISTURB EVER sign to stick on the toilet door. Then people know not to knock when I'm busy.

I borrowed the sign from Will's bedroom when he wasn't looking. The sign used to say DO NOT DISTURB, so I added EVER to make sure people took it very seriously.

But today I wasn't in the bathroom to write up case files. I was looking for Libby Smith. She wasn't there...but my secret boss was.

I stomped three times.

She stomped twice.

I stomped once.

"What's the password?" she asked.

"Children's Police Force."

"Have you finished the case yet?"

"Sort of," I replied.

"What is THAT supposed to mean?" my boss snapped. "Is Libby Smith mean or not?"

"Libby doesn't smile or play with anyone. She doesn't speak properly, just mumbles stuff. Everyone thinks she's mean but..."

I tried to say Libby was mean. I had

all the proof I needed. All I had to do was write my case file and store it under my bed. One day my boss might take the case to school court. Libby would be found guilty and get detention.

So why did I feel so bad?

"Hurry up!" my boss shouted. "I've got Science in ten! Is she mean or not?"

"I don't know...I need more time."

"No way! You've had since Monday! If we're not done by Friday, I'll have to work over the weekend. I *hate* doing that..."

"Just one final test," I said. "By tomorrow, we'll know if she's mean or not."

"You've got one more day, you hear me?"

"Very loud and very clear."

I gulped quietly so she wouldn't hear how nervous I was.

Libby didn't smile, speak or play with others. That all showed she was mean, but a tiny part of me wasn't so sure...

Then I remembered the staff room. Jimmy had told me to check it out, but now it was too late to go there. Afternoon breaktime was over. Next time out of class would be home time.

If I went to the staff room after school, Dad would ask why I was late and want to know what I was doing. He'd be angry when he found out I was sneaking around after school, especially in the teachers' private room.

Because it was so late in the day, I had to find Libby tomorrow instead. I wasn't happy about leaving the case unsolved for another day, but I had to be patient. Rushing just messes things up. If I messed up the case, I wouldn't get any juicy grapes.

On my way to the playground, I started thinking about the best time to catch Libby. If I looked for her at breaktime or lunchtime, the teachers would be in the staff room on their break. I'd be caught and get into serious trouble.

So, I had to check the staff room when the teachers were busy in class. It would be a great time to catch Libby alone.

Little did I know that Libby and I wouldn't be alone in the staff room tomorrow. Someone else would be there too. It was someone who could kick me off the Children's Police Force, and ban me from school forever…

Chapter 7

The next morning, Libby Smith still wasn't in class. The only places she could have been hiding were the staff room and Mr Badal's office. Mr Badal hadn't let anyone study in his office since someone spilt juice on his new carpet.

"Mya, is everything all right?" Mrs Cherry asked. She'd noticed me staring at Libby's desk. "Would you like to come up here?"

I went to Mrs Cherry's desk, taking

my schoolbag with me. I needed what was inside.

"I know this is hard," Mrs Cherry said quietly. "Having a new student, especially when she's *different*, can be challenging."

"I'm worried about her," I said. "She doesn't talk or smile or anything."

"Yes, well she's…" Mrs Cherry fell silent. "She'll be okay."

I reached into my bag and pulled out some colouring books and pens.

"Is that for me?" Mrs Cherry asked, smiling.

"No, you only get gifts at the end of the year."

I showed her the colouring books.

"I brought them for Libby. To show we can be friends."

"Really?" Mrs Cherry flipped

through the books quickly. "Poor Libby thought that you didn't like her..."

I wasn't expecting that. Libby was the mean one not me, right? So why did she think that I didn't like her?

Maybe she was lying. Sometimes Angel told lies so people felt sorry for her. She even pretended to cry so other kids got told off.

"I don't know why Libby thinks that," I said. "Anyway, I wanted to give her the colouring books before she came back to class."

"Great idea! These books will make her feel much better." Mrs Cherry gathered the books and placed them on her desk. "Now Libby won't be so nervous...Not nervous, I mean anxious...No, not anxious I mean...Never mind. She'll be just fine."

Mrs Cherry looked very sad. I could tell she felt sorry for Libby. She probably didn't realise that Libby was a mean girl.

"Um, I'd like to give her the books myself," I said. "She should have them right now so she isn't nervous anymore. Where is she, Miss?"

"She's—"

"Is she off sick?" I asked.

"Well—"

"Is she in another class?" I leaned in closer. "Is she at home? Did she go on holiday?"

"Holidays during term time? Mr Badal would be furious!"

"Is Libby so smart that she got moved up a year?"

"Well—"

"Or maybe she's finding work too hard, so she got moved down a year?"

"I—"

"Miss, do you know where Libby Smith is?"

Mrs Cherry looked very confused. That was my fault. I'd asked too many questions too quickly. A police officer should only ask one or two questions at a time.

"Well, Mya, Libby is in the staff room. She is...helping us tidy the place. You know how messy some teachers can be!" She laughed, but her laugh sounded fake. Just like when Mum fake laughed at Dad's bad jokes.

"I'll take the books to her," I said. "She'll feel better."

"No, it's fine here for now."

"She needs them now. I can take them. You're too busy to do it."

"Mya, darling, you are too busy too."

I shook my head. "I'm not busy. I have finished my classwork. All twenty questions."

"Okay. Well, check—"

"Over the answers," I interrupted, which was a bit rude. "Checked my work five times. The answers look right to me."

Mrs Cherry's eyes narrowed. Her teacher senses were tingling so hard I could feel them. Maybe I'd been too obvious? Well, it was too late now.

"Mya, why do you want to leave the classroom so badly?"

Uh oh. I'd been too obvious.

"Mrs Cherry, I...Um..."

Think of something, I thought. Think of something fast!

I couldn't ask to use the toilet. We'd just started the school day. I couldn't cry and say I missed my parents. That only works when you're much younger. I was eight, almost nine. Too old for that crying stuff.

Then I remembered Mrs Cherry saying Libby was nervous. Maybe I could use that info to get out of class?

"I'd like to give Libby the books now so she can feel less nervous. I could talk to her about making friends."

"I'm not sure if she'll be able to..."

"I know some people are scared when making friends. My mum says distractions can be helpful when we're scared. She says a distraction helps us focus on something good instead of something scary."

"Your mother is a wise woman," Mrs Cherry said. "The colouring books might distract Libby when she's afraid. It'll be a massive help when she's feeling really nervous."

"Distractions help my big brother too," I said. "Will distracted himself with music when he got into trouble. It made him feel better after my parents took his phone, laptop and games console away."

"He must have been very naughty."

"He was," I said. "He still is."

"Hopefully distractions will help Libby too. She's a lovely girl, but her nerves..."

Things were going well! Mrs Cherry wasn't questioning me anymore. She was thinking of Libby instead.

"Okay, Mya," Mrs Cherry said, "you can take the books to her but you must come back here *asap*. Something very important is happening soon and I'll be announcing it to the whole class."

I knew exactly what was happening soon. It was something that scared lots of kids every year. I didn't mind, though. That very important thing would help me solve this case. But first, I wanted to know what Libby was up to.

I went straight downstairs and stood outside the staff room. I couldn't go in yet. I was so excited I could barely breathe!

I'd heard that the staff room was really cool and lots of fun. Only a few lucky kids were allowed inside. When they came out, they were so shocked by what they'd seen.

One girl said the teachers had a massive TV with a million channels on it. On rainy days, teachers could stay inside and watch the best cartoons.

Another girl said the teachers had a microwave that cooked an extra-large pizza in only sixty seconds! Even better, there was a big dishwasher so no one had to wash the dishes.

One lucky boy spent a whole week in the staff room. He said the teachers' chairs were so comfy that he fell asleep in them.

I could see why teachers liked being in the staff room at breaktimes. I was so jealous! I wanted to eat pizza, watch cartoons and sleep in the staff room too. Instead, all I could do was close my eyes and imagine the best staff room in the world.

But I didn't have to imagine the staff room anymore. Now I was going to see it myself!

I knocked twice on the staff room door. I couldn't wait to go in. My heart was beating so fast!

"Hello?" I said. "Anybody in? Miss or Sir? Anybody?"

I heard voices, but they were coming from classrooms nearby. I could also hear Mandy the receptionist next door. She was typing so loudly on her laptop.

"Hello?" I knocked again, louder this time. "I've got something for Libby Smith!"

Mandy stopped typing.

Seconds later, she peeked out of her office and smiled at me. She always had the biggest smile at school. Her teeth were as white as paper.

"Mya, isn't it?" Mandy cried. "What a pleasure it is to see you again! How can I help?"

Mandy always remembered names and faces. That's what people loved about her most. She always made us feel special.

"I'm here to see Libby Smith." I held up the colouring books. "I have...her birthday presents."

Mandy tucked her wavy, jet-black hair behind her pale white ears. She looked at the books and clapped her hands.

"That looks like fun!" she squealed. "Unfortunately, Libby is away at the moment. You can leave those goodies with me and I will ensure that she gets them. I promise!"

"No, that's okay," I said. "I'll bring them another time."

"Have a lovely day, weekend and year!" Mandy said. "See you again real soon."

She slipped back into her office. Her fingers started typing away again, faster than before. Poor Mandy. Mr Badal always gave her lots of work and a short amount of time to finish. It wasn't fair!

"Off I go," I said really loudly. "Back to class..."

There was no way I was going back to class. First, I still had to ask Libby if she was mean or not. Second, I wanted to see the staff room. I wanted to try the comfy chairs, eat the tasty pizza and watch a cartoon or two before I left.

So, I quietly turned the door handle and slipped inside...

Chapter 8

The staff room was okay, I guess.

Goose bumps spread across my arms because it was so cold. I touched the radiator and it felt like ice, so I rubbed my hands together to warm up. While I warmed up, I took a good look around.

There was a sitting room area. The TV wasn't widescreen like the one we had at home. It was very small. It'd be hard for everyone to see unless some people sat on the hard, wooden floor.

Four teachers could fit on the sofas. I'd heard the cushions were so comfy that people fell asleep on them. They looked like normal, boring cushions to me. I couldn't see what all the fuss was about.

The kitchen area wasn't much better. I'd heard that the microwave cooked an extra-large pizza in only sixty seconds...but that was another big lie. The microwave wasn't even big enough to get a medium-sized pizza in. It only had a few buttons and none of them said Pizza on it. Our microwave at home had so many buttons we still hadn't used them all.

I couldn't understand all the stories about the cool staff room. So many kids had said it was so much fun in there, but it all looked really boring to me. It was disappointing, but it wasn't important right now. I was supposed to be looking for Libby, not a TV, microwave or comfy cushions.

I couldn't see any of Libby's stuff. I didn't know if she'd be back soon or not. I couldn't wait around. I had to get back to class!

She might be in Mr Badal's office, I thought. I hope not!

If she was with Mr Badal then I was stuck. How could I get into his office and talk to her? He was the bossiest, fussiest teacher ever. That's why he was the headteacher. He was bossy enough to tell all the other teachers what to do.

"My office is a mess right now," Mr Badal's loud voice boomed from the corridor. "Let's try the staff room. The other students are in class at the present moment, so we should have peace and quiet in there."

I couldn't hear the other person's voice.

"Well, young ladies first."

Were they coming into the staff room? Right now? But students weren't allowed in without permission! I'd be in serious trouble!

I had to hide!

I squeezed under the coffee table, but it was too small. My legs were poking out. I had to try somewhere else.

What about the windows? I was on the ground floor. I wouldn't get hurt climbing out.

But there wasn't enough time! The door handle was turning. Mr Badal would come in any second now. I didn't have enough time to unlock the window, open it and climb out.

I spotted a closet in a corner of the room. I rushed over and jumped inside just as Mr Badal walked in. I quietly closed the door and breathed a sigh of relief.

"This is a nice place to relax before you return to class," Mr Badal said. He sounded nervous. I'd never heard him sound nervous before. "We can talk more in here without those noisy children disturbing us."

I opened the door a crack and saw Libby sitting beside Mr Badal on the sofa. He handed her a glass of water and she sipped it. I couldn't believe my eyes, so I rubbed them and looked again. Was she friends with HIM? How could she be friends with someone so mean? Maybe because she was mean too?

A loud bang came from outside. Libby jumped, almost dropping the glass. Water spilt on the floor. I knew Mr Badal would go mad. He was Asian but his skin changed to dark red when he got really mad. I waited for him to explode!

But he didn't.

Libby buried her head in her hands and Mr Badal patted her on the shoulder.

"There, there," he said. "It's just water."

I think she mumbled, "Sorry" but it wasn't clear.

"I'll mop it up," he said softly. "We don't want it smelling of damp in here. The place smells bad enough already."

When he turned away, she grabbed him by the sleeve. He knelt beside her and said, "It's okay. I'm not leaving you. I'll get the mop and return immediately."

I pulled the door in, watching him through a really tiny gap. First he went to the staff room door and hung up his coat. I thought he would go out to get a mop. Instead, he turned and headed straight for the closet.

I looked over my shoulder. Behind me was a broom, wet wipes and...a mop. A mop! He was coming for the mop!

I backed further into the closet and held my breath. I hoped he would turn away, but he kept coming closer.

I tried to hide in the shadows, but there was a light bulb hanging over my head. If he pulled the string, the light bulb would come on and he'd see me.

I had nowhere to run. Nowhere to hide.

He's coming, I thought, and I'll be in serious trouble...

Chapter 9

Mr Badal was about to walk into the closet. Once he found me, I'd probably get detention and spoil my perfect school record. He might even kick me out of school forever.

When my parents found out, they'd take away all my police tools including my police badge, case files and handcuffs. Just the thought of losing my badge almost made me cry!

"I hope the mop is still there," Mr Badal said to Libby. "Is it that hard to return something after you've used it? Some people are so selfish!"

He reached out to the closet door.

I held my breath, keeping perfectly still.

He grabbed the door handle.

I trembled, my teeth chattering.

Suddenly there was a really loud scream outside. Mr Badal spun round and dashed over to the window. He threw it open and leaned out.

"What on earth are you two doing out there? How dare you play around at this time of hour? I want to see you outside the staff room immediately."

The naughty pair said something back, but I couldn't hear it clearly from inside the closet.

"If you needed the toilet, why are you outside? There is NO TOILET in the playground!"

They said something that made his face turn beetroot red.

"Your parents will hear about this! Inside! Now! Both of you!"

He slammed the window shut so hard I was surprised it didn't break. In a huff, he marched back towards the closet.

Closer and closer, step by step, he stomped over until he was inches away. He reached out and grabbed the closet door handle.

"Mr Badal!" Mandy cried. She walked into the staff room, smiling like always.

"What is it now, Amanda?" he asked, tapping his foot.

"Mr Badal, Dixon Davis and Daria Davis are outside your office. Should I send them in?"

"No. Let them wait out there. I am busy at the moment."

"Understood."

Mandy hurried out and closed the door quietly.

Mr Badal placed a hand on the closet door knob. I hoped and prayed and wished so hard that he would just go away.

Then Libby mumbled something.

"What was that?" Mr Badal rushed over to her. "Say it again, please."

Libby repeated herself. I still couldn't hear what she was saying.

"You're right. I'll throw some paper towels on it," he said. "No need to waste time mopping up. The whole place needs a thorough cleaning anyway."

Mr Badal got some paper towels from the kitchen area and dropped them on the wet patch. Then he sat with Libby on the sofa.

Mr Badal gave lined paper and a pen to her before sitting back. I'd never seen him so relaxed before. Why did he only act that way with her? Was it because she was mean like him? Maybe mean people liked being friends with each other?

"I'm going to give you a little test," he said. "I'll say a word and we'll see if you can spell it. You'll get bonus points if you know what the word means. You can speak if you feel comfortable or just write everything down."

Libby bit her lip, looking very nervous.

"Okay, let's begin," he said, "can

you write down how to spell the word cat?"

She waited a bit before writing.

"How about spelling the word house?"

She wrote on the paper again.

"Let's try the word badger."

She wrote it down and looked up when she was done.

"What about the word dump?"

Straight away, Libby wrote it down.

Mr Badal looked over the paper, his eyes widening. He clapped and smiled. Not the fake smile he gave to teachers he didn't like. A real, warm smile that almost made him look friendly.

"All spelt correctly and every definition is just perfect...Now let's try some harder ones." Mr Badal rubbed his smooth chin in deep thought. "I've got three very hard words this time: clover, thrifty and freight."

Libby closed her eyes a moment before writing quickly. Mr Badal watched every word, nodding proudly.

"Well done," he said when she was finished. "I'm sure you are wondering what the point of this mini test was."

Libby stared at him blankly. She didn't smile or frown. Her face didn't seem to change unless she was sad or scared.

"I was curious, that's all," he said with a shrug. "Mrs Cherry said you do not participate in lessons. I was wondering if you were struggling academically."

Libby hung her head in shame.

"But I can see that you are just as

smart as the other kids in class, possibly even smarter. And clearly you can write. Is speaking to others the only problem you have?"

She nodded, turning away from him.

"I know speaking is hard," Mr Badal said. "I used to be shy too. People thought I was mean, but really I was just nervous around others."

Libby looked surprised for a second. Then her face was blank again.

"Did your nerves make you spill the water earlier?" he asked.

She nodded.

"Let me get this straight. You find it hard speaking to people?"

She nodded.

"You are also sensitive to loud noises, just like the loud bang we heard outside?"

She nodded again.

"And you are also highly intelligent."

Mr Badal's eyes lit up.

"Based on what you've told me today, I believe you have a particular speech condition. Unfortunately, I cannot recall the name. Was it autism? No. Something related to it though..."

Mr Badal took out his mobile phone and typed something in. He flipped the screen and showed Libby a video. The volume was low, so I couldn't hear what they were watching. Whatever it was, Libby nodded along before burying her face in her hands.

"I thought so," Mr Badal said. "I will start doing more research and see how we can help you, all right?"

Libby whispered something to him.

“Do not worry about the other children. I am sure they like you very much.”

No, we don’t! I thought.

It wasn’t a nice thing to think, so I felt guilty afterwards…

“I can see why you are so upset. People like you tend to worry more than others.”

Libby nodded, wiping a tear from her cheek.

“Libby, I believe you are a thoughtful, considerate person. Someone kind like you will have no problem making friends. Just give yourself more time. There’s no need to rush!”

I couldn’t believe my ears. Mr Badal thought Libby was kind? She was so sneaky she’d even tricked the headteacher! I thought he'd see her mean side, but she'd hidden it too well.

If Libby could trick teachers, she was much smarter than I thought. Mean and smart.

Well, she wasn't smarter than me…

A good officer always thinks ahead. When the bad guys relax, they slip up. Then the officer catches them in a trap.

Right now, Libby was very relaxed. She thought she'd won. With a headteacher on her side, she could do anything. Maybe even take over the whole school!

I had to stop her before it was too late. A mean person shouldn't run a school. It was bad enough having Mr Badal there. We didn't need TWO mean people telling us what to do.

If I proved she was a mean person

then everyone would help me stop her. We could also stop other mean people like Angel and her friends. That would be great! A school full of nice people. No mean people allowed.

There was a knock on the staff room door. Mr Badal huffed and stormed over. He threw open the door.

"This is outrageous behaviour," Mr Badal barked. "Running around in the playground when you should be in class...Did I ask you to speak? SILENCE, young man!"

Mr Badal turned back to Libby and calmly said, "This will take a few minutes. Excuse me." He stepped outside and closed the door.

Libby knelt on the floor and placed the paper on the coffee table. She started writing, her eyes glued to the page. As long as she kept looking down, I could sneak right past.

I couldn't go out the staff room door. I'd walk right into Mr Badal and get yelled at with the other kids. I couldn't stay in the closet all day. I had to get back to class before Mrs Cherry sent someone after me.

There was only one way out: the window. We were on the ground floor, so climbing out would be easy and totally safe.

Getting to the window was the hard part. I had to reach it without Libby seeing me. If she saw me, she'd call Mr Badal back in and I'd be in serious trouble.

But if I distracted Libby, she wouldn't see me. Then I could sneak over and climb out the window without being spotted.

What could I use to distract her? Maybe the TV? Yeah, if I had the remote control, but that was sitting on the TV. Who leaves the remote on the TV? What's the point? You'd have to get up to change the channel.

"There has to be something else in here I can use," I whispered. "What do teachers keep in the staff room? Some snacks, I guess. Water, maybe. I don't know..."

I peeked outside the closet. Libby was still writing. Mr Badal was still moaning. Poor Mandy. I couldn't understand how someone so nice could work with someone so mean.

I looked around the room and spotted the kitchen cupboards. Maybe there was something inside I could use to distract Libby?

I slowly opened the closet door wide enough for me to squeeze through. I hoped the door wouldn't squeak because Libby might hear it. Luckily Mr Badal started shouting even louder at the students, so Libby wouldn't hear me moving around.

"This naughty behaviour is UNACCEPTABLE," he said. "You should know better at your age. How old are you? Eleven or something..."

I could hear a boy's quiet voice before Mr Badal shouted again.

"Nine years old? Oh. Well, nine years is old enough to know better!"

I crawled across the floor with the colouring books and pens I'd brought with me. Every couple of seconds I'd stop and listen out. If I could hear

Libby writing, I'd crawl a bit further. When she stopped writing, I stopped too so she wouldn't hear me moving.

Finally I reached the kitchen area. Below the tiny microwave were cupboards and drawers.

Quietly, I opened the drawers one by one. Inside were knives, forks and spoons. I couldn't use any of those to distract Libby. I had to keep looking.

When I closed the last drawer, I accidentally pushed too hard. It slammed shut.

Libby stopped writing. All she had to do was stand up and look behind the sofa. Then she would see me.

Luckily Mr Badal started shouting again.

"Young lady, I find it very hard to believe that you were outside fighting monsters," Mr Badal said. "ANYWAY, I will not tolerate anyone loitering outside...You don't know what loitering means? Well if you'd stayed in class you would know, young lady!"

Libby started writing again.

Get going, I thought. I don't have much time!

I moved on to the cupboards and peeked inside. There was nothing exciting behind the first door. Just washing up liquid, a sponge, a bucket and a stinky bin.

Behind the second door was a large Lost and Found box. Inside was a fluffy toy rabbit, scarves, woolly hats, jumpers, trainers, exercise books, water bottles, an empty lunchbox and three pencil cases.

What could I use to distract Libby?

What would keep her busy long enough for me to get out?

Quietly, I searched through the box. I thought about using the fluffy toy. It was a rabbit with the cutest ears. I gave it a quick hug before putting it back. I knew the toy rabbit wasn't alive but...I felt bad about using it to sneak out. I didn't want Libby to be mean to it when I'd gone.

I also thought about using the clothes. Maybe if I wrapped a scarf around my head Libby wouldn't recognise me.

But she'd still call Mr Badal. He'd check the school cameras to see who'd gone into the staff room. My face wasn't covered when I'd gone in, so he'd see who I was.

I need something else, I thought.

Keep looking!

Then I looked at the pencil cases. Inside one was a thick, black colouring pen. My eyes went from the pen to the colouring books I'd brought with me.

Wait a minute, I thought. I could use this…

Chapter 10

Libby was blocking my way out. I needed something to distract her with. The colouring books might work, but for Libby to see the books I needed to get her attention. How could I do that? By making a loud noise! She'd go and see what the noise was. Then I'd sneak past and climb out the window.

I had to do something fast. Mr Badal was still shouting, but he wouldn't stay in the corridor forever.

"Young lady," Mr Badal's voice

boomed, "daring to talk back to me is injudicious!"

The girl said something I couldn't hear.

"Injudicious means something is ill-advised, misguided, unwise, just plain silly. If you'd been in class instead of loitering outside, you would have known what injudicious meant!"

I couldn't sit around learning new words. I had to distract Libby! A loud noise would get her out of the way, but where should the noise come from?

I had a feeling I should go back to the closet. I don't know why. It was just a feeling. Anyway, when I looked inside I saw the mop.

If I could knock over the mop and some other things, it would make enough noise for Libby to hear. She'd get up to see what the noise was about, giving me time to sneak past.

I placed the mop on the edge of the bucket and gently pushed the bucket. The mop fell off but I caught it.

That was just a test. Time for the real thing.

Next, I placed the mop and broom on the edge of the bucket. I held my breath when I let go, hoping they wouldn't fall off yet. If they did, I'd be caught by Libby!

Slowly, very slowly, I backed away from the closet and left the door half-open. If I closed it, I wouldn't be able to carry out my plan.

My plan was to slide something across the floor into the closet. It would bang into the bucket, knocking the mop and broom off. They'd crash to the floor, making lots of noise. Libby would go over to see if someone, or something, was in the closet.

Next to the closet, she'd find the colouring books. I would write her name on them using the black marker I found earlier. Then she'd know the books were for her.

While Libby stood there flipping through the books, I would sneak past. I'd climb out the window and run back to class without getting caught.

So, step-by-step, my plan was:

1. I make a loud noise in the closet.
2. Libby goes over to investigate.
3. She sees the colouring books and looks through them.
4. I sneak by her and climb out the window.
5. I go back to class and hope Mrs

Cherry doesn't tell me off for taking so long.

"This plan is SO simple," I whispered. "So simple it can't go wrong!"

I crawled back to the kitchen cupboards and wrote Libby's name on the colouring books. I tucked the books under my arm for safe keeping.

"Now I need something to slide or roll across the floor."

I took out the lunchbox from the Lost and Found box. The bottom was nice and smooth. It was perfect for sliding across the wooden floor. It would slide right into the closet and knock everything down, just like a bowling ball knocking down pins.

With the lunchbox on the floor, I kept my eyes on the closet and didn't look away. I'd learned that from tennis players on TV. They always kept their eyes on the ball.

Always keep your eyes on the target, they said. If you take your eyes away for a split second, you might miss...

"Don't look away. Don't blink. Don't miss."

After a deep breath, I pushed the lunchbox across the floor. It slid for one second and stopped.

You've gotta be kidding me, I thought. Why didn't it slide more?

I picked it up and rubbed the bottom with my sleeve. It definitely wasn't bumpy or dirty. Why wasn't it sliding properly?

I tried again. Like before, it only slid for a second. It wouldn't go anywhere near the closet.

I returned the lunchbox to the Lost and Found box and took out a water bottle. Nice and round, it was perfect for rolling. I felt silly for not trying it first.

I lined up the bottle with the open closet and imagined it rolling right inside. With my eyes fixed on the closet, I hoped for the best and rolled the bottle.

The bottle slowly rolled across the floor. It rolled into the closet and headed straight for the bucket. I got ready to crawl away before Libby came over.

But the bottle had other plans.

Just before it hit the bucket, it rolled slightly to the left and out of sight.

I couldn't believe it! I'd been so close!

Stay calm, I told myself. Do what Daddy says. Just try again and again until you get it right.

So, I grabbed another water bottle and rolled it. This one turned much sooner and stopped by the door.

Aw come on, I thought. That's worse than last time!

My hands started shaking. I only had one bottle left. If I messed up again...

I picked up the last bottle. I stared at the bucket and imagined the bottle rolling into it.

"Knock that bucket," I whispered to the water bottle. "Please!"

Just as I pushed it away, Mr Badal shouted. It made me jump, so the bottle rolled off to the right. I held my breath, trembling. If it rolled too far, Libby would see it!

I got ready to run and jump out the window. I didn't care if she saw me. I had no choice. I just didn't want to be there when Mr Badal got back.

Shaking from fear, I watched the bottle roll away. I kept hoping it would stop.

When it finally started to slow down, it was too late. The bottle gently bumped into the wall.

Libby stopped writing.

I started sweating, my hands clammy.

Libby got up and walked over to the bottle. I peeked round the sofa and watched as she stared down at the empty bottle. Her face wasn't confused or scared or anything. It was just blank.

I stared at her.

She stared at the bottle.

I started shaking.

So did she.

I gripped the back of the sofa, my nails digging into it.

Her hands clasped together, trembling.

Please don't see me! I thought. Don't see me! Don't see me! Don't see me! Don't see me! Please!!!!!!!

Her head slowly turned towards me and stopped. I ducked behind the sofa, crossing my fingers and toes. Had she seen me? I was about to find out!

Her footsteps edged closer and closer. Then they stopped. I felt her close by. I kept perfectly still. I held my breath.

Then her footsteps got further away. When I peeked out, she was writing again. This time, her hands were shaking.

"One more thing," Mr Badal snapped. "Remember, I have important matters to attend to and work to do. Unlike you naughty children, I enjoy working very hard!"

I didn't believe him. No one likes working hard because, you know, it's hard. People only like hard work when it's finished. That's when you realise it was worth it.

"I have an important business meeting," Mr Badal said. "Speak quickly. I have to go."

He was coming back! I had to go right now!

I grabbed a pencil case. It was round like the water bottle. I could try rolling it across the floor, but what if Libby saw this one too? She'd know someone else was in the staff room.

Mr Badal was coming back soon. I had maybe a minute or so. Then I would be in the WORST trouble of my school life. Maybe my *whole* life.

Throw the pencil case, I thought. Just do it!

Before I could get ready, my hand just threw the pencil case. It all happened so fast.

Too fast.

Before throwing the pencil case, I should've taken one more look around. I didn't realise at the time, but I hadn't followed my simple plan. I'd forgotten to do something very important...

Chapter 11

When I threw the pencil case at the closet, everything happened so fast!

The case flew through the air. It slipped past the closet door, squeezing through the gap, and smacked into the mop. The mop fell over, pushing the broom down. They both fell off the bucket, clattering in a messy heap.

When Libby got up, I quickly crawled down the side of the sofa and waited until she'd reached the closet. Then I ducked behind the sofa where she'd sat earlier. The window was close by.

I waited for her to spot the colouring books. Then I could sneak out. The books should've been on the floor near the closet but...they weren't there.

That's when I realised the mistake I'd made.

I'd forgotten to leave the colouring books over there. I'd brought them with me by accident!

She was peeking in the closet, slowly edging inside. I had to get the colouring books over there before she turned around. I still had time if I was quick.

Before she turned back, I tiptoed over there and placed the colouring books by the microwave. I left one book close to the edge, hoping it would get her attention. Then I rushed back to my hiding place behind the sofa.

The room went quiet. Too quiet. I had to see what she was doing.

I peeked out and saw Libby by the microwave. Slowly she flipped through the colouring books. After glancing at the closet, she picked up the books and turned around. I ducked just before she saw me.

A moment later, she sat down on the sofa I was behind. I peered over when she started colouring. It was strange being so close without her knowing.

"I have had enough of you naughty twins," Mr Badal shouted. "Return to class immediately. I will speak to your parents about this."

Get out, I thought. Mr Badal is coming!

Slowly I opened the window. A cold breeze blew in, but Libby didn't stop colouring.

I slipped out the window. When my feet touched the ground, I stood there and took a few deep breaths. My heart needed to slow down a bit before I went back to class.

Then something strange happened...

As I tiptoed away, I thought I heard Libby say something. It was very, very quiet, but she definitely said something. It sounded like "Thank you".

Thank you? Was she thanking me for the colouring books? But how did she know I was there? I'd been very careful. I'd kept hidden and only peeked out when she wasn't looking.

No way, I thought. She couldn't

have seen me.

And it just didn't make sense. Why would a mean person say thanks? Mean people are rude. They don't say nice things like "Thank you" and "Your welcome". Mummy says polite people say those things. Mean people are not polite.

Or maybe Libby hadn't said anything. Maybe I'd imagined her speaking. Daddy said I was really imaginative.

Whether Libby had seen me or not, I was late for class. I had to get moving!

Students need a good reason for leaving lessons. There was NO good reason for being in the playground during class time. That's why I had to be very careful on the way back. I hid a lot and moved fast so I wouldn't be spotted. Luckily I didn't bump into any teachers or students.

A minute later, I was back in class.

"I almost sent out a search party," Mrs Cherry said as I walked in. "What took you so long? Is everything all right?"

No. I was still shaky after being stuck in the staff room with a mean girl and a mean headteacher.

"I'm fine, thanks!"

The teachers thought Libby was some shy girl who couldn't speak. I had to prove she was mean, not shy. Then everyone would know she could talk but didn't want to.

I went to my desk and sat down. There was more classwork to do, so I got started. It wasn't long before Jimmy poked me in the arm.

"Hey, Mya," Jimmy whispered. "How'd it go?"

"I might be in trouble," I said. "I'm not sure."

"Well, I've got some bad news..."

Libby must've seen me in the staff room and told on me! Had Mr Badal called Mrs Cherry? Was I being kicked out of school? Would I lose my police badge?

"Tell me quickly," I said. "How bad is it?"

"My top secret sources say..." He leaned in closer. "We have to give speeches again. I have no idea what to talk about this time!"

Bad news? This was GREAT news!

At our school, students had to give a short speech each term. I'd been practising at home for months. I was ready.

No one but Angel and I liked giving speeches, but Mrs Cherry made sure everyone took their turn.

Angel loved giving speeches. For five whole minutes, she was the centre of attention. We HAD to look at her. We HAD to listen to her. Ignoring a speech lost points off your mark. So far, I'd had straight As. I wanted to keep it that way.

When it was time to give the speech, Mrs Cherry took names out of a floppy hat. If she said your name, you went next. No exceptions. No excuses.

In the past, people had tried to go later. "I forgot my speech," one girl said. "Can I go next year?"

"No, you can go now," Mrs Cherry replied.

Another girl tried using the "My fish ate my speech and homework" excuse, but Mrs Cherry didn't fall for that either. Everyone knows only dogs eat homework, not fish.

"Can't give the speech," a boy said. "I think I'm gonna be sick!"

"Nice try," Mrs Cherry said. "I've heard that excuse before."

Unfortunately, this time he wasn't lying. It was pretty gross...

My point is, Mrs Cherry said whoever got picked had to go up next. If not, you got a U grade. The U means Ungradable. Ungradable means you failed.

Everyone in class had to give a speech. Everyone in class meant Libby Smith would have to give a speech too!

My plan was simple: Make sure Mrs

Cherry took Libby's name out of the hat. Then Libby would *have* to say something to us or she would fail her first speech...

Chapter 12

We were in the playground after lunch, but I couldn't play with my friends. I was too busy getting ready before our English lesson.

The speeches were starting today. Mrs Cherry would probably let Libby skip her speech. Libby would be the only one who didn't have to say anything. Then people wouldn't know she was as mean as Mr Badal.

Libby and Mr Badal were probably working together. Now I had someone working with me: Jimmy. He'd help me get inside the classroom while it was empty. I couldn't do that on my own. If I messed up and got caught, I'd be in serious trouble...

I looked around to make sure no teachers were watching me. No students were looking either. Good. I didn't want anyone to see me go inside.

Jimmy was across the playground, playing football. He kept looking at me. He was waiting for my signal.

I waited another minute, just in case a teacher came out. None did, so I nodded at Jimmy. He nodded back.

Jimmy took the football and kicked it as far as he could. It flew over the fence and bounced off three cars in the school car park. One car alarm is noisy, but three are really, really loud!

Everyone else ran over to the fence to see what was happening. If the car alarms didn't get the teachers' attention, a big crowd of kids definitely would.

"What on earth is going on?" Mrs Tipple scurried over. She was the youngest-looking teacher we'd ever seen. When she first came to school, we thought she was a student. Then we saw her driving off to lunch. Kids don't drive. I'd love to drive, but Dad said no.

"Everyone, line up immediately!" Mrs Tipple cried. "Someone tell me what the commotion is about, please."

Now everyone was distracted by the car alarms. No one was watching me.

I crept inside and waited in the toilets.

When Mrs Cherry and some other teachers ran outside, I raced upstairs to our classroom. I knocked, just in case someone was there, but no one answered. I slipped inside and quietly closed the door behind me.

Empty classrooms are so creepy. I always feel like someone might be hiding under a desk, waiting to jump out and say, "Boo!"

And it's hard to be good when no one else is around...I could take all the tracing paper I liked. And some glitter. Maybe some pretty card paper too. I could even move the clock forward a minute or two.

Or three or four or five...

It wasn't worth it, though. If I got a bad school record, I could never work in the Children's Police Force again.

"Let's get to work," I told myself. "I don't have much time."

My pencil case was in my drawer where I'd left it. Behind it was a plastic bag full of names my brother Will printed off for me. He wasn't helping me for free. I'd spent all my money paying Jimmy, so Will was taking half my grapes instead.

"Half?" I'd cried. "But...but...but why HALF?"

"Because you need me," Will said, squeezing his teenage spots. "Pay up or get lost."

Mean cow! I wished I had a big sister instead! Sisters are always nice. I should know. I'm a sister.

Losing half my grapes was bad, but worth it. Now I could set a trap to catch Libby!

I stayed away from the windows as I crept over to Mrs Cherry's desk. I didn't want anyone to see me from the playground.

"Please be open," I said.

I pulled out Mrs Cherry's drawer. Usually she locked it, but this time it was open because she'd left in a hurry!

"Where's that floppy hat? There it is!"

Sitting on the register was the speech hat. Inside were thirty names printed on thirty pieces of paper. Each paper was folded in half. Mrs Cherry would open each one and read the name inside.

I tipped the names into the bin. I replaced them with the names Will had printed off for me.

By "names" I really meant ONE

name...

The car alarms stopped.

"Time to go," I said. "Everyone's coming back now."

I ran to the upstairs toilet. I waited there until everyone had gone past. Then I slipped out and followed Mrs Cherry into class.

"Take your seats quickly," Mrs Cherry snapped. "No time-wasting! Hurry!" She wiped the whiteboard, getting ink on her hand. I ran up and offered her a tissue.

Why? you ask. Because I had to.

A good police officer gets along with other people. You never know when you might need someone's help. Having a teacher on my side might get me an adult police job quicker. Then I could work at a police station with other officers.

"Thank you," Mrs Cherry said, taking the tissue from me. She blew her nose in it and went to the bin.

That's when I realised my *huge* mistake!

The names from the speech hat were still in the bin! I'd forgotten to cover them with tissues or paper. Now Mrs Cherry would see the names. Then she'd check the speech hat.

"Who switched the names?" she'd shout. "Who did this?"

I would be too scared to own up to it. Jimmy wouldn't talk either. A very angry Mrs Cherry would check the school cameras and see me sneaking inside.

"I'm very disappointed in you," she'd say. "You are a very naughty girl!"

Mrs Cherry would give me detention. Then she'd tell my dad. He'd tell my mum. My very angry Mum would take my police badge away!

Things would be even worse when I got back to school. I'd have to tell my secret boss that my badge was gone.

"You can't solve cases without a police badge," my boss would say. "You aren't a REAL police officer anymore. No more cases for you! And no more grapes either!"

The Children's Police Force would kick me out. I would cry. Will would laugh at me. I'd cry even more.

"Um, Mya," Mrs Cherry looked confused. "Are you okay? You've been standing there daydreaming for a while now..."

"Yes, Miss," I said, trying to smile. "I'm fine."

No, I wasn't.

I can't get into trouble, I thought. I can't...No, I WON'T lose my police badge or grapes!

I couldn't let Mrs Cherry put the tissue in the bin. To stop her, I had to do something really gross...

Chapter 13

"Mrs Cherry! Stop!"

Mrs Cherry froze. "What's wrong?" she asked.

I had no choice. There was only one thing I could do. It made me sick thinking about it, but I couldn't let her see the speech names I'd dumped in the bin!

I held out my hand.

"Can I have the tissue back, please?"

She laughed, so I asked again. She stopped laughing then.

"But, why?" she asked. "I've used it!"

"I want to...recycle it."

"You cannot recycle a used tissue." She dabbed her pointy nose again, her furry eyebrows twitching. "Didn't you do your recycling homework?"

"I...don't have any more tissues."

"Then go to the toilet and get some."

She turned back to the bin, so I ran ahead and held out my hand again.

"Mya Dove, go and sit down!"

"My mum gave me that tissue. You know she's a night nurse, right?" I forced out a tear. "I don't see her all day because I'm at school. At night, she's at work. She takes care of the babies at the hospital. That tissue has her perfume on it."

"Aw, poor thing!" Mrs Cherry

pinched my cheeks. "The tissue means you can smell her perfume whenever you miss her. That's beautiful. So sweet."

Her eyes were watery, so tears were coming soon. That meant my plan was working.

"Okay, Mya. Here you are, darling." She placed the soggy tissue in my hand. I wanted to drop it, but I had to hold on tight. "Now please sit down."

I couldn't be sick or she'd put the speeches off. Thinking of my juicy grapes, I held on to the snotty tissue until I got to my seat. Then I held on a bit longer because Mrs Cherry was still watching me. All I could do was hope that the big booger stuck to my hand didn't dry there.

"Class, today is the big day," Mrs

Cherry cried. "Can you guess what we'll be doing?"

No one said a word. Some people weren't even looking at her. One boy looked like he was going to be sick.

"Oh, come on," Mrs Cherry said. "You all knew this day was coming. I have been dropping hints for a week or two."

Angel looked around the room with a big smile on her face. She couldn't wait to be the centre of attention.

"Okay, class," Mrs Cherry said. "I'll spell it out for you."

Mrs Cherry started writing on the whiteboard. I watched Libby's face as she read the word SPEECH. She bit her lip and looked down at her desk. Her body was shaking and I could hear her teeth chattering. People said she was mean but...she looked like she needed a big hug.

I felt sorry for her, but why? I wasn't supposed to feel sorry for mean people.

"Remember," Mrs Cherry said, "this exercise will be graded. It is ten per cent of your total mark for the year. Everyone will do the speech. No exceptions will be made..." Her eyes stopped on Libby, who was sweating. "Of course exceptions will be made under certain circumstances."

Everyone looked back at Libby, who was sweating so much her coily afro hair was wet. It was sticking to her face. She started rocking back and forth like she'd pass out.

"Are you ready, class?" Mrs Cherry shook the speech hat. The paper rustled inside. "Who is going first, I wonder?"

Mrs Cherry reached into the hat and pulled out a name. She frowned when she saw it.

"This is a mistake," she said. "I must have mixed up your names with another class." She slipped the name into her pocket and reached into the hat again.

Out came another paper. She unfolded it and frowned. I knew why. It was because she'd picked the same name again.

"Libby Smith?" she said quietly.

Libby froze. She held on to her desk, sweating more and more.

"Class, Libby was not told that we give speeches at this school. We will give her more time. Next term, not now."

Mrs Cherry reached in again and pulled out the next name. She turned bright pink, now sweating herself.

"...Libby Smith?"

She reached in again and again and again. Libby's name came up again and again and again.

"I must have duplicated some names, class. Excuse me one moment."

Mrs Cherry dug around in the hat, opening name after name after name. Over and over, she looked confused.

"Mrs Cherry," Angel said, standing up, "you said NO exceptions. It's not fair if Libby skips her speech! If she skips it, so will I!"

There were a few quiet voices that agreed with her. I wasn't one of them.

"Angel White, sit down," Mrs Cherry snapped. "I am busy at the moment."

"No, I will not sit down. No one else got extra time before giving a speech." Angel turned back and glared at Libby. "She can say *something*! Just talk. Talking is EASY. Just open your mouth and words come out!"

Libby opened her mouth, but no words came out. Instead, a tear trickled down her cheek.

"Can't she talk at all, Miss?" Angel spat. "Not even for thirty seconds? If we're doing five minutes each, she can do thirty seconds! That's easy-peasy!"

Mrs Cherry looked around the classroom. There were lots of angry faces.

People got so nervous giving speeches. They didn't want to do it. They *wouldn't* do it if Libby didn't.

"Libby, can you come up here, please?" Mrs Cherry said. "Just for thirty seconds."

Libby slowly went over and stood in front of the whiteboard. Tears ran down her cheeks, her lips shaking. She mumbled something I couldn't hear.

"Scaredy-cat!" Angel shouted. "Didn't want to play with us in P.E.? Bet you're sorry now!"

"Stop being mean," said Ahmarri. He used to be really quiet too. "She's shy."

"Yeah, leave her alone!" Jimmy cried.

"No!" Angel snapped. "Libby's mean and I hate her. We ALL do!"

Libby ran out the door in tears. Mrs Cherry stormed over and shouted at Angel. The class whispered to each other, everyone looking really guilty.

Jimmy leaned over, an angry look on his face. His cheeks turned bright red like his spots.

"Not cool, Mya," he said. "You said she's another mean girl like Angel! You were wrong. They're totally different."

"But my secret boss said she's mean! I'm just doing my job, okay?"

"Well, I'm not helping you with this case anymore," he said. "I feel bad enough already."

"How'd you think I feel?"

I kept thinking of Libby crying. They didn't look like fake tears. They were real. She wasn't faking it to trick us. She was really sad.

And it was my fault.

"Whatever, Mya," Jimmy said. "Good luck with the case. Enjoy your reward for making her cry. I hope the sweets are worth it..."

He didn't know I was getting paid in grapes. I didn't want to be teased for liking grapes more than chocolate and sweets. Some kids just don't understand how tasty grapes are. Broccoli is nice too.

Now I wasn't excited about getting my grapes. They looked so juicy, but when I imagined eating them, I felt guilty. I kept thinking of Libby crying her eyes out.

Was she going to run away from school? Maybe run away from home too? Would she move schools? Would we ever see her again? If not, I could never say sorry. Somewhere out there she might hate me forever and ever and ever...

Now I felt really down. Even cried a little when no one was looking.

I feel so bad, I thought. How can I feel better?

Saying sorry to Libby would help, but she wasn't around...

How else could I feel better? By talking to someone about the case. They'd help me figure out where I'd gone wrong.

I couldn't talk to Jimmy because he was still angry with me. I couldn't talk to my secret boss because she was too mean. There was no one else at school I could talk to about the case, so I decided to try someone at home instead.

After school, Mum would be very busy getting ready for work. Will was mean, so he wouldn't help unless I paid him first. Will's cat couldn't help because cats don't solve cases. Well, ours didn't anyway. Fortunately, there was someone else I could talk to...

Chapter 14

Back home, I felt even worse. Not knowing if Libby was okay made me feel guilty. All that shaking, sweating and crying she did wasn't a "mean girl" thing.

It also got me thinking: Was *I* the mean girl? I'd been mean to Libby all week. I guess *I* was the mean girl the whole time, not her. I was mean, just like Angel. Libby hadn't done anything wrong.

I got changed from my school

clothes into my home clothes: a comfy t-shirt and baggy shorts. Then I went downstairs to the garage and knocked on the door.

"Who is it?" Dad asked.

"Detective Inspector Mya Dove." I had my police badge ready to show him. My badge number was 180289. "I need your help with a case. Open up, Sir!"

The door was open, but police officers need permission to go into other people's rooms and houses. If I didn't follow the rules, the case wouldn't be accepted in school court.

"Detective Inspector, please come in."

I rushed inside and stopped by our car. The bonnet was up and the engine was purring like Will's cat. My dad's legs were poking out from under the car. I squeezed his shoe and he laughed.

Remember, officers must be nice to people. If my dad didn't trust me, I'd lose his help and advice. He was really old (forty-five years old), so he had lots of experience and great advice to share.

"Sorry, Detective Inspector, I couldn't pick you up today because this darn car is playing up again." He knocked something metal and the car hissed. "Did Will get there on time?"

"He was two minutes late! I could've been anywhere when he finally got there! You know some naughty kids like to wander off. Luckily I behaved and waited patiently for him near the school gates."

"Apologies, Detective Inspector."

"I already said you can call me

Detective Dove for short."

"That would be easier." He reached out and grabbed a torch. "How can I help the case?"

"Everything you say will be top secret, but if we go to school court, you'll have to test...testi..."

"Testify."

"Testify before a...um..."

"Testify before a jury of my peers. I accept those terms."

I didn't know what "peers" meant. I'd look it up later.

"Can you hand me a wrench, please?"

I got one from the toolbox and handed it over. He went back under the car. I could hear the squeaky bolts he was tightening.

"Mr Dove, two weeks ago, a new girl

came to my school. Everyone thinks she's mean. Do you understand?"

"No."

"What don't you understand, Daddy? I mean, what don't you understand, Mr Dove?"

"You said this girl is mean, but why is she mean? What makes her mean? What did she do that's so mean?"

"She didn't smile at people, even when they smiled at her. Mean!"

"Not really. Some people are just very serious-looking. They don't smile a lot, but they're still nice people...if you give them a fair chance."

I thought about it. Did we give Libby a fair chance? She'd had three weeks to be nice, but that wasn't very long. Maybe she needed more time?

Could my secret boss be wrong?

Libby not smiling didn't mean she was mean. Maybe she was just a bit...

"Shy," Dad said. "Maybe she is shy. Does she spend most of her time alone?"

Every day in the playground she was alone. In the lunch hall, she sat alone. In P.E. she sat out every game. Even after school, she'd walked out alone with her head down.

Was she alone at home right now?

"We've got shy people in class, but they talk when you talk to them. She just mumbles and cries."

Dad came out from under the car. He looked sad. I wiped the oil stain off his cheek.

"Detective, do you remember your cousin Ebony?"

Nope.

"She sounds like your friend—"

"Libby isn't my friend."

"Do not interrupt. It is rude!" He pulled me down onto his lap. "It sounds like Libby has social anxiety, just like your cousin Ebony."

"Social anxiety? So, they're just shy?"

"It's a lot more serious than shyness." He took out his mobile phone from his overalls and went online. "Here. Let me show you..."

Dad and I read lots of websites about social anxiety. They made me feel sorry for Libby. Anxiety was a hard thing to have.

"We'll read more about it tomorrow, okay?" Dad said. "I'd better get back to work on this car."

I left Dad and went upstairs to my

bedroom. It was packed full of police stuff like books, gadgets and toys. Instead of looking over old case files, I took out my speech notes and started practising for tomorrow.

"This speech will get me another A," I said. "Angel will be so jealous!"

I pulled out the police toolbox kept under my bed. Inside was equipment like a magnifying glass, handcuffs, rubber stamps for case files, and a fingerprint kit.

"What should I take for my speech tomorrow?" I wondered. "Or should I print out some pictures instead?"

I was SO excited about giving my speech. I'd been practising for weeks and weeks and weeks.

But I shouldn't have bothered.

The great speech I'd worked on for

so long wouldn't be heard. Instead, I'd be giving a speech that no one, not even me, was expecting…

Chapter 15

On Friday morning, everyone was still talking about Libby Smith. When we lined up in the playground, she wasn't there.

"Maybe she ran away from school," Ahmarri said.

"No way," Eve said. "I heard she's staying in Mr Badal's office forever...or until we leave school in Year Six."

Jimmy kept giving me angry looks. I tried speaking to him, but he stuck his fingers in his ears and turned away.

"I feel so bad," said Emma. "I shouted at Libby when she followed me around. Where do you think she is, Mya?"

"Maybe she's in class," I said. "She could be waiting up there for us."

I was wrong. The classroom was empty. When we sat at our desks, Libby's stayed empty. No Libby, no pencil case, no schoolbag. Nothing.

"Despite what you may have heard," Mrs Cherry began, "the speeches will continue as planned. No exceptions will be made...unless you are very nervous."

Mrs Cherry's eyes were on Libby's desk.

"I know giving speeches is scary, but you have nothing to worry about. Just do your best, okay?"

Some people nodded. Others looked even more scared.

"Teachers get nervous too," Mrs Cherry said. "My first speech was a horrible experience, but over time I improved. Practise doesn't make us perfect, just better. That's all that matters."

When she reached for the speech hat, several people started trembling. One girl's teeth were chattering, her face covered in sweat. I'd never realised how scared some people were of speaking. Speaking didn't scare me at all. I was only scared of spiders.

"You poor darlings," Mrs Cherry said, her cheeks bright pink. "Public speaking is feared by millions of people. It's not right to force anyone to give a speech."

"Does that mean we don't HAVE to give a speech?" Emma asked.

"It's up to you all," Mrs Cherry said. "Class, almost everyone is nervous before giving a speech. However, being *extremely* scared isn't normal. Do any of you feel shaky, teary or sick?"

A few hands went up.

"I will not force anyone to give a presentation, but I expect a written report instead. If possible, please TRY giving a speech. With more practise, you'll feel less nervous over time."

Mrs Cherry picked up the speech hat. She pulled out a name and looked over at me. I went to the whiteboard and took out my speech notes.

Everyone but Mrs Cherry groaned.

"Not this again," Angel said.

"Police, police, police! I'm tired of it!"

"Silence," Mrs Cherry snapped. "If Mya wants to give another presentation on the police force, she may do so. You are free to speak about whatever you want."

Okay, fine. It's true that I always gave speeches on the police, but there's just so much to say!

One time I explained how to put on handcuffs and how not to lose the key (very important!).

Another time I talked about how to plan a police investigation. Good officers know how to question bad guys. They also know how to dust for fingerprints.

I could've talked about police work for years. Sure, sometimes I repeated myself, but what can I say? I loved my job so much!

My speech notes were typed and each heading was highlighted in yellow. I'd timed the speech to finish in exactly four minutes, so I'd have a minute to answer questions. I'd even brought pictures from a real police case. It was the case of a thief at the local sweet shop. He stole ten chocolate bars before he was caught!

"Mrs Cherry, boys and girls, today I'll—"

The door opened slowly and Mr Badal popped his head in.

"Sorry to interrupt but..."

He opened the door wider and Libby was standing there, her eyes to the floor. She quickly walked in and went to her desk. Instead of putting her schoolbag down, she kept it on her desk and hid behind it.

"Thank you, Mr Badal," Mrs Cherry said. "Mya, please continue."

I checked the clock so I could time myself. Then I started again.

"Mrs Cherry, boys and girls, today I'll talk about a very serious crime that happened in a local shop. It took the police over three days to find out who the thief was. By the time they found him, he'd eaten all the evidence...or so he thought!"

I turned to my next note.

When I looked up, Jimmy was staring out the window. Nobody had ever done that to me before! Other students would at least *pretend* to be listening, even if they were bored. Jimmy had to be VERY angry if he wouldn't even look at me for five minutes.

"The, um, police checked the cameras and saw ten-year-old John Brown taking sweets without paying for them. The town was very angry. If everyone else has to pay for sweets then John should too."

I turned to the next note and looked up.

I saw Libby.

She was at the back, looking at her pencil case. She looked at me for a second and looked away. The longer I watched her, the guiltier I felt.

She was sad because of me.

"Mya?" Mrs Cherry asked. "Is there a problem?"

I shook my head and then nodded. Feeling guilty feels bad. The only way to feel better is to make things right, but how could I?

When I looked at Jimmy again, I wondered if he wasn't really angry. Maybe he was disappointed? He was disappointed because I'd been so mean to Libby.

Then I remembered what he'd said to me days ago: "Being a good police officer means being a good person. Don't forget that."

That's how I could make things right. That's how I could make Libby feel better. All I had to do was be a good person.

"Mya, is there something you'd like to say to the class?" Mrs Cherry looked worried about me.

It was time to choose.

I could be a good police officer and talk about the sweet shop thief. It was a very interesting case!

Or I could be a good person and help Libby. Then she'd feel better. Jimmy wouldn't ignore me anymore. I wouldn't feel guilty anymore.

"We haven't got all day!" Angel cried. "Say something!"

"Be quiet, Angel." Mrs Cherry glared at her. "Mya is remembering what she has to say. Be patient."

People were staring at me. Jimmy was still looking outside, pretending not to care. Libby peeked out from behind the bag on her desk. Mrs Cherry glanced at the clock.

What's more important to me? I wondered. Being a good person or being a good police officer?

Do I want to be nice like Jimmy or mean like Angel?

Make a decision, I thought to myself. You've got to choose!

"Mrs Cherry, I have something very important to tell everyone." I took a deep breath. "It's about Libby Smith..."

Chapter 16

"Your speech is about Libby Smith?" Mrs Cherry's eyes widened, her furry eyebrows twitching. "I don't understand. I thought your speech was about the sweet shop case?"

I shook my head. Then I nodded. I threw my hands up, not knowing what to do.

Angel and her mean friends laughed at me. I gave her an angry look. She stuck her tongue out at me.

"Is she talking about something

new?" Angel cried. "Good! I'm bored with her police speeches. It's always the same thing."

"I wasn't talking about the police. I was talking about the sweet shop robbery."

"That again?" Angel rolled her eyes. "You told everyone about it the day after it happened!"

"It's different this time! I have photos!" Oh, I hated Angel so much! "And I have a witness statement! An old lady saw the whole thing!"

"That's enough, ladies," Mrs Cherry said.

I turned back to Mrs Cherry. Angel and her friends giggled behind my back, but I didn't care.

"Why are you changing your speech now?" Mrs Cherry asked. "It is a tad late. I would advise you to finish what you started."

"No, Miss," I said. "Libby is going to be my speech topic. She's more important than John Brown stealing sweets."

"I don't think this is a good idea..."

"I HAVE to do this," I said. "My friend reminded me that being a good person is important. If I don't give this speech, I won't be a good person."

Jimmy looked at me, his eyes narrowing. I hoped he wasn't still angry.

"Continue if you must," Mrs Cherry said, "but if Libby becomes upset then you must stop. I hate to see students cry."

I looked at each person. I did that to make sure everyone was paying attention. They needed to hear what I had to say. It was very important.

"Today I am going to talk about...social anxiety," I said. "Social anxiety is like shyness but bigger. Much bigger! It makes normal people like you and me really nervous when they do stuff with others. They could be nervous when answering the teacher, asking for help or looking you in the eye. Some socially anxious people even find it hard to smile!"

Libby was watching me closely. So was Jimmy.

"Shyness goes away by itself. Social anxiety doesn't. Children and adults with social anxiety need help, but the anxiety makes it hard for them to ask."

"Do they only feel nervous when speaking?" Mrs Cherry asked.

"No," I said. "They might feel nervous just *thinking* about speaking because they're scared of saying something silly or wrong."

"I understand," Mrs Cherry said. "They're nervous not only when speaking but also when socialising with others. It must be even harder when there are many people around."

"It is. Speaking to one person makes them nervous. Speaking to lots of people makes them very, very nervous!"

That's why Libby started crying when she gave her speech. Talking to thirty people must've been so scary for her.

"Being in groups can upset socially anxious people," I said. "They're left out when everyone else is talking. It makes them feel like they don't belong."

"I hope no one here feels that way," Mrs Cherry said, looking around the classroom. Her eyes stopped on Libby. "Every student belongs here. Every single one of you."

Libby mouthed, "Thank you" to Mrs Cherry. Mrs Cherry smiled, tears in her eyes. I felt a bit weepy too, but I had to keep speaking. I wasn't done yet.

"We must be patient, extra patient, with socially anxious people. They're NOT mean. They're *scared.* Staying away from us doesn't mean they don't like us. They stay away because it makes them feel less nervous, but being alone doesn't help them get better."

"So, Mya, what *would* help?" Mrs Cherry asked. Everyone leaned in to hear my answer. "How can we be supportive?"

"Don't force them to talk. They'll do it when they're ready," I said. "And tell them it's okay if they say something wrong. We all make mistakes."

"Yeah, whatever," Angel mumbled. "Maybe SHE just doesn't like us!"

"Stop judging people you don't know," I said. "It's a mean thing to do."

"YOU judged her too!"

"Yes, I did." I looked over at Libby. "I'm sorry."

"What're you sorry for?" Angel rolled her blue eyes. "She doesn't talk because she's mean. End of discussion!"

"She doesn't speak because she's NERVOUS," I said. "Speaking doesn't mean you're nice. You're proof of that. You talk all the time and you're mean."

"You can't talk to ME like that!" Angel spat. "I'm telling my—"

"Enough, Angel," Mrs Cherry snapped. "Does anyone else have any questions?"

Jimmy put his hand up. He didn't look angry or disappointed anymore.

"Okay, yeah, so how do we know one when we see one?" Jimmy asked.

"One?" I glared at him and he blushed.

"Sorry! I meant a socially anxious person. What do they look like?"

"They might be serious-looking. They might not smile a lot. They could have a blank face."

"By blank face you mean they're expressionless," Mrs Cherry said.

"Expressionless means they aren't showing emotions like happiness or sadness."

"So that's how they look, but how do they act?" Jimmy asked.

"They're alone a lot. They might mumble or stay quiet. Sometimes they look nervous, sometimes they don't."

"I'm never nervous," Jimmy said quickly. "When my...*friend* is nervous, he's shaky. Doesn't talk right. His throat feels all tight. He might sweat a bit."

"Socially anxious people feel the same way," I said. "The words can feel like a lump stuck in their throat."

"Good questions, Jimmy," Mrs Cherry said, writing something down. "Anyone else?"

Angel put her hand up.

"Anyone else?" I asked.

"Mya!" Mrs Cherry tutted. "Go on, Angel."

"Thank you, Mrs Cherry." Angel gave her sweetest smile to Mrs Cherry before giving her coldest glare to me. "Mya?"

"What?"

Mrs Cherry tapped her ruler on the desk. If it was a normal schoolday, I would've told Angel what I really thought of her. I couldn't do that now because my speech was being graded. Being naughty would get me a B, spoiling my perfect speech record of straight As.

There's nothing wrong with a B, but…an A is better, you know?

"Nice to see you again, Angel," I said like the sweetest girl in the world.

"Do you have a question?"

"Why can't SHE just get over it? Like, who's scared of talking? Losers!" She laughed. No one else did. Not even her friends. "What a scaredy-cat!"

Libby started breathing really quickly. Tears rolled down her cheeks. Angel glanced back at her and shrugged. That made me so mad!

Look, I respected my jobs (student and police officer), but sometimes doing the right thing is more important than solving cases or getting good grades. I'd be doing the right thing by helping Libby. I'd be doing the wrong thing if Angel got away with being rude. If I got a B grade then too bad!

I marched over to Angel's desk. She leaned back, her eyes widening. She looked at Mrs Cherry for help.

"Mya, calm down," Mrs Cherry said. "And Angel, please behave yourself!"

"Sorry," Angel said with a grin.

"You're *not* sorry," I snapped. "I won't let you bully Libby anymore."

"Is SHE your friend now?" Angel sniggered. "Then tell your friend to get over her anxiety stuff! Scaredy-cat!"

"Her name's Libby, not SHE! LIBBY can't just get over her social anxiety, but she will beat it with our help!"

Libby wiped away her tears. She stared at me, her eyes wide open. I couldn't tell if she was scared or surprised. It didn't matter. I just wanted her to know that I cared.

"Angel, we've all got something that scares us. Speaking scares Libby. Big, hairy, evil spiders make me cry. Angel, you're scared of—"

"Don't say it!" She sank under her desk. "I trusted you!"

"Bunnies."

Everyone, even Libby, burst out laughing.

"You don't get it," Angel whispered, still hiding under her desk. "The fluffy tail...The whiskers...Acting all cute and cuddly. It's a trick! They're really evil!"

"Okay, whatever..."

I left her there and went over to Libby.

"Libby, we understand if you're not ready for a speech yet. We'll help you practise speaking, right guys?"

"Yep," Jimmy said. "Just wave me over!"

"Ahmarri and I will help too," said

Emma. “He’s really quiet like you, and very nice to everyone. Libby, I bet you’re nice too.”

Ahmarri waved and Libby waved back.

“And sorry about the other day,” Emma said. “I shouldn’t have shouted at you. I’ll never do that again, I promise. If you’re lonely you can always follow me, okay?”

“And me,” Ahmarri said quietly.

“And me,” Jimmy cried.

“And me,” said the rest of class. Except Angel, of course.

There were tears in Libby’s eyes. Were they happy tears? Yes! She was happy! We all were. Except Angel, of course.

“Libby,” I said, “if you can’t answer questions yet, you can write things down and I'll read it out for you."

Without thinking, I reached out and hugged her. She looked so surprised, but she hugged me back. Everyone but you-know-who clapped for us.

Libby and I sat down. Jimmy smiled at me. I smiled back. It was nice having him as a friend again.

Angel was still hiding under her desk, but nobody cared.

"Class, we don't have enough time to give all our speeches today."

A few people cheered.

"However, next week speeches will go ahead as planned. If you are too nervous to speak, submit a written report instead."

People cheered even louder.

"For now, let's do comprehension. Please turn to the fifth chapter. Read through and answer the questions at the end."

I opened the textbook and tried to read but couldn't focus on the words. Usually reading was easy, but my mind was still buzzing after my speech.

"Hey Mya," someone whispered behind me. "Your boss wants to see you before lunch!"

I couldn't wait to see, I mean *hear* my secret boss again. I'd solved the case and was excited about eating my juicy reward.

Very soon I'd get not one but TWO big surprises.

One would be very good.

The other, very, very bad...

Chapter 17

"Mrs Cherry?" I said, putting my hand up. She hurried over and bent down beside Libby and me. Jimmy had swapped places with her so we could work together. "We've finished early. Can I go pee? I'm desperate!"

"Of course," she said. "When you're done, go straight to lunch."

Libby waved goodbye. I really wanted to stay with her, but I had to close the case.

I'd never been so excited about

going to the toilet. Each step took me closer to my juicy green grapes. I couldn't wait to eat them!

When I reached the bathroom, I waited by the door just in case someone was there. I didn't want mean girls like Angel hearing about my top secret cases.

The bathroom door opened a bit. No one walked in.

"Who is it?" I asked.

"Your boss!" she snapped. "Get into the toilet stall. Now!"

I went into the first toilet stall and locked the door.

The bathroom door flew open and my boss walked past. She slipped into the toilet next to mine and slammed the door shut.

I stomped my foot three times.

My boss stomped twice.

Then I stomped once.

"What's the password?" my boss asked.

"Children's Police Force," I said.

"Good...Now say sorry."

"For what?" I asked.

"You were late. I had to wait here for thirty seconds."

"Sorry, I had lots of reading to do. The questions were pretty hard."

My poor stomach grumbled. It was almost lunchtime. I was very hungry. Thinking of those juicy grapes made me even hungrier!

I reached under the stall and held out my hand. It was time to get my reward! I couldn't wait to eat my bouncy, sweet, juicy green grapes.

"Um, hello!" My hand was still

empty. "Give it!"

"No. No grapes for you."

"But why?" I didn't want to cry but...

"The case was about proving Libby Smith is mean or not."

"Yeah, so?"

"Because of that social anxiety thing, we still don't know if she's mean or not."

"She's been nice so far," I said, my stomach grumbling. "I think we're friends now."

"The deal is off. The case is closed. No grapes. Go to lunch."

Usually I did whatever my boss said, but these were grapes we're talking about. I'd been looking forward to them all week!

"No grapes at all?"

"No."

"Aw, come on!" I cried. "That's not fair! You won't even give me ONE grape?"

"No."

"Not even my bonus grape?"

"Fine...Take it."

The brownest, yuckiest grape I'd ever seen rolled across the floor. It stopped by some damp toilet tissue.

"Eat up," she said. "Don't waste good food!"

I didn't eat the grape. Honest!

Instead, I went straight to lunch. Libby was sitting with my friends. There was a seat beside her for me, so I sat down and opened my packed lunch.

Peanut butter sandwiches. Yum!

Libby kept looking at me. I wasn't

sure what to do, so I just kept eating. She moved her chair closer to mine and waved me over. I leaned in so I could hear her better.

She mumbled something. The other kids were too loud, so she repeated herself. I still didn't catch it, so we went into the hallway.

"What'd you say?" I asked. "It's so noisy in there! All that talk. We're supposed to be eating, you know?"

"Um...Thank you." Her hands were shaking a little. "For being nice to me."

"No problem," I said.

I was the first kid at school she'd spoken to. It made me feel really special!

"Can I ask you something?" I asked.

She nodded.

"Did you see me in the staff room

yesterday? You know, when you talked to Mr Badal?"

She nodded.

"I should practise sneaking around," I said. "I don't want mean people like Angel to catch me, you know?"

She nodded again.

"Well, at least you liked the colouring books I left."

"Can we...colour together?"

"Of course we can!" I said. "I just got some new pens last week. I have all the colours in the rainbow. Plus black and brown."

Because she'd been so brave by talking to me, I decided to tell her my big secret: I was a police officer working on top secret cases at school.

"A *real* police officer?" she whispered.

"Well, sort of. Not really. No." I showed her my badge. My mum bought it for me last Christmas. "Cool, right?"

"...Could I help you someday?"

I stopped to think about it.

Libby was so quiet. She could sneak into a classroom and hide without anyone noticing. That meant she could spy on bad guys and hear their biggest secrets.

"If the right case comes up, I'll let you know, okay?"

"Thanks!"

When lunchtime was over, we went outside and played together. I couldn't believe how much things had changed! On Monday, Libby was the mean girl. By Friday, she was my friend.

I would've loved some green grapes, but having a new friend was a billion times better! Grapes couldn't help with homework, play games, come over for sleepovers or talk about police cases.

Libby could do all that and more.

If I hadn't given her a chance, I would never have known what a great person she was. Just like my grandma said: "Never judge someone by the opinion of others." Others thought Libby looked mean, but she was really nice. I should've ignored the silly rumours about her.

You never know what others are going through, I thought. Don't judge who you don't know.

There were hundreds of students I didn't know. So many faces and names I didn't recognise. I wondered what their lives were like. I might never know. What I did know was that I'd give EVERYONE a fair chance to be my friend.

But what if someone didn't want to be friends? What if they turned out to be mean like Angel? Well...so what? So what if someone was mean! I didn't have to be their friend and they didn't have to be mine. Not everyone would like me and that was okay.

Nobody likes everybody.

Instead of forcing mean people to like me, I'd just stay with nice people.

Nice people like Jimmy.

Nice people like Libby.

Nice people like me.

And nice people like you.

CASE CLOSED

Dear Reader

Hello, I hope you enjoyed my book. You can email me at contact@zuniblue.com. I'd love to hear from you!

I'd really appreciate it if you left a book review saying whether you loved it, hated it, or thought it was just okay. It doesn't have to be a long review. Thank you very much!

Keep reading to get your 100 free gifts...

About the Author

Zuni Blue lives in London, England with her parents. She's been writing non-fiction and fiction since she was a kid.

She loves telling stories that show how diverse the world is. Her characters are different races, genders, heights, weights and live with various disabilities and abilities. In Zuni's books, every child is special!

Solve More Cases

Would you like to read another case file?

Mya doesn't share her cases with just anyone, but she knows she can trust you.

Keep reading for more top secret cases she's solved...

The School Pet Who Went Missing

Mya's school has a brand new pet. It's cute, cuddly and loves everyone. Unfortunately, it's gone missing! Did it run away? Or was it stolen?

To solve the mystery, Detective Dove must face her bossy headmaster, a mean prefect, and a sneaky teacher with a dark secret...

The New Boy Who Hears Buzzing

The new boy's ears are buzzing. He must've been bugged, but who did it? Was it a student? A teacher? Or some bad guys?

To solve the mystery, Detective Dove must face the detention kids, a crafty inspector, and some naughty officers at the police station...

The Parents With A Sleepover Secret

Mya has to stay at her enemy Angel's house. Angel is forcing her to solve a tough case. If the case isn't solved, Mya will be kicked off the Children's Police Force!

To solve the mystery, Detective Dove must face an angry poodle, a scary garage, and the meanest girl in the universe...

The Fat Girl Who Never Eats

Ten school burgers were stolen. Everyone blames the fat girl, but no one saw her do it. Is she the burger thief or is it someone else?

To solve the mystery, Detective Dove must face her crafty dad, a strange caretaker, and the shocking secret in the school basement...

Dedications

This book is dedicated to anyone with social anxiety, particularly selective mutism. I know how hard it is to live with.

Thank you to my family and friends. I appreciate all the love and support you have given me. I couldn't have done this without you.

An extra special thank you to every reader who's emailed me. I love hearing from you!

100 Free Gifts For You

There are 100 FREE printables waiting for you!

Certificates, bookmarks, wallpapers and more! You can choose your favourite colour: red, yellow, pink, green, orange, purple or blue.

You don't need money or an email address. Check out www.zuniblue.com to print your free gifts today.

Printed in Great Britain
by Amazon